The Boy Who Saved
Christmas

Shelagh Moore

ILLUSTRATED BY GARY WING

Other books by the same author...

The Little Reindeer
Shelagh Moore   £4.99
978-0-9928029-2-9

The Plastic Warrior
Shelagh Moore   £4.99
978-0-9928029-5-0

The Lost Dinosaur
Shelagh Moore   £4.99
978-0-09928029-1-2

Available on Amazon now:
https://www.amazon.co.uk/Shelagh-Moore/e/B0034O6F08

© Shelagh Moore 2020
ISBN: 978-0-9928029-3-6
Illustrations, Gary Wing
Design and print origination, Charles Design Associates

For permission to reproduce photographs, the author and publisher gratefully acknowledge the following: Dreamstime photo library for images appearing on: pp 20–22.

Many years ago, in a far off land of snow and ice, a poor boy, dressed in hand me down furs, walked through the forest. It was a crisp, clear evening and the moon shone brightly on the snow making it gleam and sparkle. He was from a place called Utsjoki in the very north of Lapland.

He lived in an old log cabin with his mother on the edge of the forest. He worked for his uncle looking after his reindeer herd. He was a boy with little to show to the world but a kind and caring heart.

A reindeer had wandered from the herd and the boy who was called Reinhart which meant Brave one, had been sent to find him. Reinhart wasn't feeling very brave, he knew there were wolves coming into the area and was worried in case they were near. He had to find the reindeer and return him to the herd by tomorrow.

As it was Christmas Eve he was also looking for some branches with berries on them to take home and decorate for Christmas Day as a surprise for his mother. Suddenly, he heard the plaintive cry of a reindeer in distress. He stopped and listened carefully. There it was again – the cry of a young and very worried reindeer. The one he was searching for!

Reinhart followed the cries and soon found himself in a clearing in the forest.

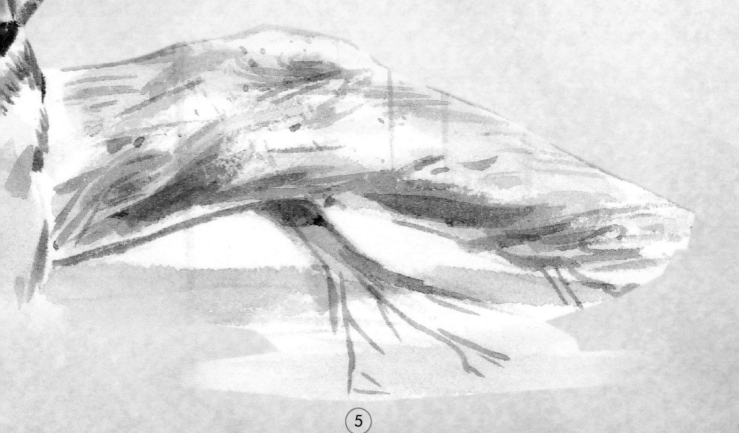

The reindeer had caught an antler in the low hanging branches of a fir tree.

On the far side of the clearing, in the shadows a lone wolf was crouched watching the reindeer. Lifting his head and stretching his neck, the wolf took a deep breath and howled loudly. An answering howl returned his call. It sounded nearby.

The reindeer was in great danger if the wolves came and attacked it and he had to bring it back to the herd. What to do? The boy dashed across the clearing and tried to free the reindeer.

'Stop struggling!' he cried to the reindeer which seemed to understand him as it stood quite still. As the boy jumped onto the reindeer's back, he felt him tremble.

'Quiet now,' he soothed. 'Be calm and be still, I will help you to get free.' The reindeer stood very still and the boy began to untangle his antler from the branches.

The reindeer rolled his eyes in fear as he saw more wolves come into the clearing. He was expected elsewhere that night and was late! If he was caught by the wolves he would be finished and the night would be a disaster for his master.

Reinhart worked frantically and at last the antler was loosened from the branch that was holding it. As the last small branch was removed the wolves set up a howling and started to run across the clearing. They leapt through the snow and were nearly upon them when he finally freed the reindeer.

'Run!' he screamed, clasping the reindeer around its neck and closing his eyes in fear as the wolves ran across the clearing. Instead the reindeer sprang into the air.

Reinhart had his eyes tight shut and didn't realise he was in the air. Just as well as these reindeer were supposed to be a secret! He just felt the reindeer moving under him and then suddenly there was a thud and he opened his eyes to see his cabin in front of him.

His mother opened the door and smiled. 'I see you found Prancer, put him in the shelter', she said, 'your uncle will be pleased to see him in the herd tomorrow. Then come in and eat.'

As he went in to eat, he felt sorry that he had not been able to get a branch to decorate for Christmas Day but he had saved the reindeer which was a relief.

Later that night, the reindeer landed in a clearing and ran up to a sleigh that was standing loaded with sacks of presents.

A large man in a red suit with a white beard was sitting on the sleigh looking worried.

'At last Prancer, you are very late – where have you been?' Then he saw the damaged antler and frowned. 'What has happened to you ?' he demanded in a booming voice.

Prancer explained – in this magical land they could all talk to each other and be understood. The man said to his reindeer,

' You had better get into your place, this boy must be rewarded – he has saved Christmas although he does not know it.'

In the meantime, Reinhart and his mother had eaten a bowl of stew she had made for the occasion and decorated their cabin with some tattered fir branches from outside their cabin.

'It's not much, but we have each other which is more important than decorations,' his mother told him as they hugged and said goodnight.

Reinhart felt a hand shaking his shoulder and saw a man in a red suit standing by his bed.

'You have saved Prancer and you have saved
Christmas. Now get into the sleigh, we are late and I will
need help tonight' said the man. Puzzled, he did as he
was told and when he looked from his seat on the sleigh
he saw reindeer in pairs in their harnesses waiting for
the command to run.

The man who was Santa Claus yelled 'Fly my reindeer, fly fast and high we have a long way to go tonight!' The reindeer pulled and the sleigh slowly began to move forward. Then all at once they leapt up and ran up into the sky pulling the sleigh with them. Reinhart gasped in delight, what an adventure he was having or was he dreaming?

Santa Claus let him fly the sleigh while he sorted out the presents and dropped them down chimneys and magicked them into homes as they sped by.

Sometimes they stopped and went into a house to leave a special present for a child who might need some extra Christmas magic and love. Santa Claus was very gentle when he delivered those gifts – 'Some need to know they are loved' he murmured to the boy, 'Kindness should always be shown to those who need it.'

They finished as dawn was breaking and the sleigh stopped in a clearing near the boy's home. 'Here', said Santa, 'take these branches to your mother and here is a present for you to give her. You helped save Christmas and I will always remember you, live well.'

He smiled and shook the reins and the sleigh was lifted into the sky and soon disappeared. The boy went to his house, and put the branches in their place with the present under them. He went back to his bed and slept soundly.

He was woken by his mother calling him and went downstairs, to a big hug from his mother who was delighted with the branches and her present. There was also one for him under the tree. It was a wooden statue of a reindeer with its branches caught in a fir tree.

The boy smiled to himself – so it wasn't a dream he thought as he picked up the wooden statue and saw Prancer's face grinning at him.

When he went to check the herd who should be standing there but Prancer. Reinhart went up to him and hugged him. Over all the years of his life, Reinhart remembered that very special

Christmas night and tried always to show kindness to those
who needed it as Santa Claus had asked him to.

Did you know?

Reindeer are found in the North where the Sami people live. They have been herding reindeer for thousands of years. A Roman writer called Tacitus wrote about a strange people who wore fur, herded reindeer and went about on skis in the year 98 AD.

In the 800s a chief called Otter visited King Alfred in Anglo Saxon times and told him about the Sami who managed reindeer in herds.

The Sami reindeer herders lived in groups, in Finland they were called *siiddat* and moved around the North in places like Sweden, Norway, Lapland, North Finland and Russia. These groups were made up a several families who worked together. Today there are reindeer districts in Finland

They used reindeer for food, milk, pulling their sleighs and this was their way of life for many, many years.

Today some Sami families still have their reindeer herds and others show people such as tourists what life is like in the North where they live.

Did you know?

Christmas

Santa Claus's story goes back hundreds of years to Saint Nicholas. Saint Nicholas was the bishop of a town called Myra which was a small Roman town in what is now modern Turkey. He was a gift giver and known for his care and protection of children. Saint Nicholas's day is celebrated on December 6th in different countries.

Santa Claus is now thought to live near the Arctic circle in Lapland. He delivers Christmas presents with the help of his reindeer.

Wolves

A wolf is related to the dog family or species. They live in the wild in different parts of the world. They like each other's company and live and work in packs that are made from family units. They can communicate with each other using facial expressions, we might say by pulling faces at each other. They can take up different poses, make gestures and howl to signal the beginning of a hunt or to call the pack together.

Wolves hunt in packs. They eat different animals including reindeer, moose, birds, moles and other smaller rodents. They have to work hard to feed their cubs every day and they teach their cubs how to hunt when they grow larger and can eat with the pack.

Printed in Great Britain
by Amazon